D1533353

THE CASE OF THE PURLOINED POODLE

A 1920S HISTORICAL COZY MYSTERY

THE KITTY WORTHINGTON COZY CAPERS

MAGDA ALEXANDER

Hearts Afire Publishing

CHAPTER 1

London
September 1923

THE PURLOINED POODLE

"OH, MISS WORTHINGTON. My poor Gigi." Mrs. Grimes mopped her face with a dainty handkerchief which by now was sopping wet from the many, many, many tears she'd shed. "I can't bear to think what those brutes are doing to her."

"No, indeed, Mrs. Grimes," I commiserated with her. The lady had telephoned the Ladies of Distinction Detective Agency this morning, her sobbing so extreme, her speech had been unintelligible. But finally I'd been able to understand the words—her Gigi had been kidnapped. Upon hearing such alarming news, I'd urged her to call the police, but she'd refused to do so. She wanted me to handle the matter. Hoping to convince her to contact the authorities, I'd rushed to her Belgravia address. It was only after I arrived, I

1

learned Gigi was a purebred standard poodle. Certainly, a serious matter that needed to be investigated, but at least no person had been taken.

"Gigi loves to go for walks in the park." She turned to the woman standing next to her. "Doesn't she, Bertha?"

Bertha Watkins, introduced to me as Gigi's nanny, agreed. "Yes, Mrs. Grimes. She does." Dressed in a serviceable dark blue gown, she appeared to be in her mid-forties, if her salt-and-pepper hair was anything to go by. While her mistress was a portrait of grief, Bertha was a study in worry. Her constantly wringing hands proof of that.

"Gigi was especially eager to do so," Mrs. Grimes explained, "as the day was so fine."

Except for the threatening rain and blustery wind, that is.

But that didn't stop Bertha from echoing her mistress's remarks, "A fine day indeed, ma'am." Clearly, she knew which side of her bread was buttered.

"She'd barely reached the park when two ruffians . . ." Mrs. Grimes dissolved into more tears. Waving the limp handkerchief at Miss Watkins, she said, "You explain, Bertha."

"Yes, ma'am." Bertha nodded. "As Mrs. Grimes said, I always take Gigi for a walk right after her breakfast. We'd just reached the park when these miscreants jumped from the bushes. One pushed me to the ground, the other grabbed Gigi. Before I could scream, they'd fled with her."

"There were two of them?" I asked.

"Yes. Two men."

I jotted the information on the notebook I'd brought with me. "Did you recognize them?"

"No! I'd never seen them before."

"What did they look like?"

Her hand flew to her throat. "Why, I barely got a look at them. It happened so fast."

"A rough impression would do. Sometimes it helps to close your eyes."

"Very well." She did as I suggested. "They wore workman's clothes."

"Describe them, please."

"Dungarees, in a shade of brown. They had caps on their heads. Worn ones."

She recalled more than she thought she would. "Hair color?"

"One had dark hair; the other was fair. Scuffed shoes."

"Clean shaven?"

"The fair one was, the other had a beard. A bushy one."

"Did they say anything?"

Her eyes snapped open. "No. They just stole her right out of my grasp." She turned worried eyes to her mistress. "I'm so sorry, Mrs. Grimes."

"It's all right, Bertha. You couldn't help it." Turning to me, Mrs. Grimes asked, "We'll get her back, won't we, Miss Worthington?"

First rule in investigative work, don't promise more than you can deliver. "I'll do my very best. Now, you said you received a letter."

"By morning post, right before I called you," Mrs. Grimes handed it to me.

The note was written on common paper. Although the handwriting was barely legible, the message was perfectly clear. "We have your mutt. If you want her back, you'll have to pay 1,000 pounds. We'll tell you when and where. Don't call the coppers."

"That's why I didn't telephone the police," Mrs. Grimes said. "I fear what they will do to Gigi if I do."

"That's an outrageous amount of money," I said.

"I'll pay, Miss Worthington. Whatever it takes. She's all I have." She applied the handkerchief once more to her wet cheeks. "Mister Grimes and I were not blessed with children, you see."

"I understand."

"I don't know what I'd do if something happened to her. They may keep her collar as long as I get my Gigi back."

Alarm bells rang in my head. "Her collar? Is there something special about it?"

"Oh, didn't I say?"

"No."

"It's made from 18K gold and studded with diamonds." A watery smile accompanied that statement. "Only the best for my girl."

CHAPTER 2

THE LADIES OF DISTINCTION DETECTIVE
AGENCY

*A*S I ENTERED the Ladies of Distinction Detective Agency, I was fairly bowled over by a tall, male body who smelled divine. "Lord Marlowe!"

"Miss Worthington. My apologies." He nodded before rushing off.

"What on earth?" I asked Betsy.

My former maid, now the agency receptionist, bit back a smile. "Best ask Lady Emma, Miss."

Following her suggestion, I stepped into the office of Lady Emma, my partner in the agency and a dear friend. "What on earth happened to Lord Marlowe?" Clearly, he wasn't a happy chappy.

"Isn't he the drollest?" She was laughing so hard tears were running down her face.

I glanced toward the agency's front door half expecting

him to materialize once more. "What put him into such a snit?"

Rather than answer me, she said, "He retained us as a client."

My gaze bounced back to her. "Did he really? To do what?"

"Find a tie clip he lost at Wattier's, his gentlemen's club. You've seen it. The one with the wolf's head."

"That ugly thing? Why would he want it back?" I wrinkled my nose as I took a seat on the Queen Anne guest chair across from her desk. Covered in dark blue velvet, it was a match to her own.

"A family heirloom, apparently. I asked for a twenty-pound retainer. In cash. That's what set him off."

I barked out a laugh. "You didn't! We usually only ask for five."

"He doesn't carry legal tender on him. So I wanted to see what he would do." She pointed to the door. "That was his reaction."

"You are—"

"Clever?" She offered with a grin.

"Most definitely." And mischievous, at least when it came to Marlowe, a consequence of her mad attraction for him.

"How did your interview with Mrs. Grimes go?" She asked.

Over the next few minutes, I shared the details of my conversation with the grieving dog owner.

"But why didn't she telephone the police?" Lady Emma asked once the whole sorry tale spilled out. "If my dog had been kidnapped, that is the first call I would have made."

"The kidnappers told her not to contact them. She's afraid if she does Gigi would meet an unpleasant end."

"That's horrible. Do you think they would do such a dastardly thing?"

"I doubt it. They kidnapped Gigi for the money. They're demanding one thousand pounds."

Lady Emma gasped. "That's an outrageous amount of money to get a dog back."

"That's what I said. But Mrs. Grimes has no children, no relatives. Her husband died last year, leaving her a very wealthy woman. Gigi is the one thing she truly loves."

"So, what are you going to do?"

"Call Robert, for starters." My fiancé, Robert Crawford, Chief Detective Inspector at Scotland Yard. Unlike previous months when our consults over murder investigations were rather clandestine affairs, I now had a valid reason for contacting him any time I wished. I hadn't abused the privilege during our earlier agency inquiries for they'd been easily solved. But this one was a notch above the others, if for no other reason than a large ransom was an element of the enquiry.

Lady Emma's expression showed surprise about my statement. "Are you planning to request his assistance on the investigation?"

"Oh, no. I would never dream of doing such a thing. But he might know if other dogs have been taken and ransoms demanded."

Her brow cleared up. "Ahh, I see. In that case, he may very well have some helpful advice."

"Exactly."

"And it does provide you with an excuse to see him," she said with a mischievous grin.

"You know me so well, dear Lady Emma. So, how will you handle Marlowe's request?" I asked.

"Well, we'll need someone connected with Wattier's. Any suggestions?"

"Dickie Collins." I'd met him during an earlier investigation when a murder had occurred aboard the Golden Arrow.

At the time he'd worked as a server on the train but was now employed at one of the better restaurants in the City of London, a position Father had helped him obtain. "He might know someone who works at that gentlemen's club, or someone who knows someone."

"Excellent suggestion."

"I thought so," I replied with a grin.

"What about Owen Clapham? Should I seek his assistance with this matter?"

A former Scotland Yard detective inspector, Mister Clapham had come into my life when I'd determined to learn investigative techniques. He'd not only become my tutor, but a dear friend. We retained him on a part-time basis whenever we had need for his help. But he'd be of better use in my inquiry. "No. I'll use him for the dognapping case. He's bound to know people who might have information or give us a direction to pursue."

"Very well. Should I send Dickie Collins a note?"

Dickie had proven quite useful. With a wife and a little one to feed, he was always eager to take on new assignments or consults. But you had to approach him just so. Riverside Mansions, the place where he lived, was located in a less than desirable part of town. Although the building itself was quite respectable, some of the denizens who loitered in its vicinity were not. Dickie preferred to be approached through a note to avoid raising suspicion. "Yes, do." I came to my feet. "I'm famished. Any biscuits left?"

Lady Emma's face pinked up. "Ate the last of them for breakfast. My apologies."

I squeezed her hand. "Don't. The bakery down the street should be delivering a fresh batch soon. How about we take a break at the Tea and Tattle to celebrate our two new cases?" The Tea and Tattle was not only a fine tea shoppe but a place to celebrate our victories as well as regain our bearings when matters did not go our way. It was one of the reasons we'd chosen the Hanover Square address.

Her brow wrinkled. "Do you think that's wise? After all, someone might come to our door in need of our services?"

"We won't be gone long. If something urgent comes up, Betsy knows where to find us. And then linking arms, we made our way to the tea shoppe for a much welcome respite and refreshments.

CHAPTER 3

KITTY VISITS SCOTLAND YARD

"*Y*OU'RE NOT BUSY, are you?" I asked Robert as I walked into his office. "If you are, I can go." Of course, I'd called ahead. I wouldn't barge in without letting him know first. Still, something could have come up between my telephoning him and the present.

Before answering, he turned to the officer who'd escorted me to his office. "That will be all, sergeant."

"Yes, sir."

Once the officer left, Robert kissed my cheek. "I'm never too busy for you, darling." Grabbing his fedora, he said, "I was just heading out to lunch. Care to join me? We can discuss things there."

"I'd love to." Soon, we were on our way to the Cock and Bull, a pub on St. Martins Lane in the city of Westminster which had become a familiar haunt of ours.

Luckily, the pub's private room was available, a necessity

when discussing a case. Once we placed our order, he said, "Tell me about the case."

Before doing so, I retrieved my case notebook from my handbag so I could refer to it if the need arose. "Gigi, that's her name, is a standard poodle. She was grabbed at Belgrave Square while her nanny was walking her."

He arched a brow. "The dog has a nanny?"

"As well as a groomer, and a nutrition consultant."

He barked out a laugh. "Surely, you're jesting."

I grinned. "It's all true. She was also sporting a diamond collar at the time, which explains why she was kidnapped."

He arched a brow. "A diamond collar on a dog?"

I grinned. "Nothing's too good for Gigi as far as her owner is concerned."

He shook his head. "So, what happened at the park?"

"As I said, her nanny was walking her when out of the blue two ruffians—the nanny's words—accosted her. One pushed her down; the other grabbed the dog. They were gone before she could even scream. She was that surprised. Or so she says."

"Who is this nanny?"

"Her name is Bertha Watkins. Before Gigi was adopted, she served Mrs. Grimes as a maid. Of course, I'll investigate her to see if she's acquainted with any unsavory characters. But that's not all. Mrs. Grimes, the pooch's owner, received a ransom demand in the post. They want 1,000 pounds for the return of the poodle."

He whistled. "That's a huge amount of money."

"Exactly so." I closed my notebook. "But the reason I wanted to discuss the matter with you, other than to see you, of course, was to find out if you'd heard of other dognappings."

"Plenty of pooches go missing, but this is the first time

I've heard of such a large ransom demand. I'll ask around the Yard to see what I can learn."

"Thank you, Robert. That will be a huge help." If other dogs had been taken, maybe someone at Scotland Yard could provide a lead.

While the food was served, we paused our discussion but quickly resumed it once the waiter left.

"Whoever took Gigi had to have known Mrs. Grimes is quite wealthy," I said, digging into my bangers and mash, a favorite fare of mine.

"The ransom demand would certainly support that argument."

"And there were two of them, so it was not a spur-of-the-moment decision. The kidnapping was most definitely planned. I'm thinking a sighting in the park. At some point, somebody probably noticed the sparkler around the dog's neck."

"Or it might be an inside job," he said after taking a sip of his dark ale. "Somebody in that household may be acquainted with an unsavory member of society, and together they planned the crime."

"I will be pursuing that theory," I said. "Any other thoughts?"

"Whoever took her is likely to pawn it. I would visit those shops and see what you can discover."

"Mister Clapham will be handling that task while I interview the household staff."

"Those avenues of enquiry should provide a lead or two you can follow."

"That's my hope." I shut my notebook. Both of his suggestions were things I'd already decided upon. So I was happy to see I was on the right track.

Once we finished the delicious meal, he asked, "Are you free on Saturday?"

I nodded. "What do you have in mind?"

"Well, you've always wanted to visit a jazz club."

It'd been a fond wish of mine, but with all the murder investigations, I hadn't had the time. In semi-dramatic fashion, I clutched my hands over my chest. "Be still my beating heart."

Amused by my theatrics, he grinned. "I'll call for you at nine."

"Why don't you come for supper? At eight? We can head to the club afterward." He had a standing invitation from Mother which he took advantage of as much as possible. Regrettably, it wasn't often enough as Scotland Yard more often than not claimed his time.

"I'll be there. Unless something comes up at the Yard, that is."

"Let's hope nothing does." I'd known what he was when I accepted his proposal of marriage, and I honored him for his dedication to duty. But sometimes Scotland Yard made it very difficult to conduct a courtship.

"Any other enquiries come your way?" he asked, after taking a last sip of his ale.

"Marlowe, believe it or not, visited the agency yesterday. He wanted to hire us to find a tie clip of his. A family heirloom. I think it's his way of bringing business our way. More than likely, he's doing it for Lady Emma. He's attracted to her, and yet . . ."

"Yes?" he asked when I hesitated.

"He doesn't invite her to the theatre, the opera, or anywhere else for that matter. And another thing, why did he remain in London when every other aristocrat left town in August? He has a beautiful estate where he hunts every year, and yet here he is. If you ask me, this is his way of courting her."

His lips turned upward in a smile. "I've always admired the way your mind works."

"Why, thank you, Inspector. High praise, indeed."

"Shall we ring for dessert?"

I nodded, happy to extend my time with him.

CHAPTER 4

A VISIT TO A PAWN SHOP

I'D ASSIGNED THE TASK of visiting the pawn shops to Mister Clapham. Since he'd been a Scotland Yard detective inspector, he was familiar with the merchants who traded in stolen goods. But having never patronized one before, I'd decided to join him. It would be a learning experience for me.

Our first stop was at a street in London's East End known as Thieves' Row. Clearly, not its official name.

"How did it earn that moniker?" I asked Mister Clapham.

"The criminals themselves call it such. Shopkeepers located along this route don't often bother with the provenance of pawned items. That works well enough for items of little value. But the police are not as forgiving when it comes to more expensive pieces."

"Such as the dog's diamond necklace?"

He nodded. "Exactly so."

"You'd think they would want to hide their nefarious intent. Calling it Thieves' Row clearly gives away the game."

"They ain't the sharpest knife in the drawer, Miss," Martha, a former informant of Mister Clapham, said. Since he'd be instantly recognized as a copper, he'd arranged for her to act as a prospective bride in search of a sparkler for her wedding day. Because I could in no way sound like a cockney, which she was, I was to pose as Mabel, her wedding attendant. Mister Clapham had stressed, more than once, I was not to speak as I was only there to lend credence. Best laid plans and all that.

At first, things went swimmingly. Martha made her wishes known. The proprietor showed her piece after piece, all of which she turned down with a sneer. "These won't do, ducky. Don't you 'ave something fancier in the back?" From her cleavage, she retrieved the stack of pounds I'd given her and flashed them at him. "Oi'm willing to pay."

The man's eyes grew wide when he saw the bundle. Could he have Gigi's diamond collar on the premises?

As he took a step toward the rear, the bell over the shop door rang, and a gentleman entered the shop. Well, I assumed he was a gentleman by the way he was dressed. Three-piece suit, bowler hat, buffed-to-a-mirror-shine footwear, all in the latest fashion. Unfortunately, he seemed to recognize Martha. One glance at her and he gave the proprietor the high sign. A slice across the throat.

In no time at all, the shopkeeper turned downright ugly. "Planning to grass me up? Get out of here. Both of ye."

Knowing we'd been made, Martha and I tried to squeeze past the man by the entrance. She made it. I didn't. He blocked my path before I could make my retreat.

His narrowed gaze slowly took me in. "You're no tart."

"I beg your pardon." I tried to push past him to no avail.

"A lady, are ye? What's yer game?"

Knowing he'd tweaked onto me, I decided to come clean. "We're searching for a stolen poodle."

His upper lip curled. "And you thought old Bill was 'iding 'im in the back of the shop?"

"The dog was wearing a rather expensive diamond collar at the time."

"Let her pass, Nick." Mister Clapham said. He'd been keeping a lookout across the street. But as soon as Nick blocked my path, he'd rushed forward to make his presence known.

"Thank you, Mister Clapham," I said, profoundly grateful for his help.

Nick's appreciative gaze roamed over me. "She your fancy piece, copper?"

From deep in his coat, Mister Clapham retrieved a revolver. "I said let her pass."

Smirking, Nick stepped aside. "No call to get yer knickers in a twist, Inspector. I ain't 'urt the lady. We were just 'aving a bit of a chinwag, weren't we, darling?" He flashed me a charming smile.

Which I didn't fall for. After all, I'd seen the best. "Sure we were."

I moved past him ready to leave the shop behind. But Nick's next words stopped me. "That sparkler yer searching for?"

I turned back. "Yes?"

"No money monger in the East End is fool enough to take it. They'd all loike to stay out of the clink, ye see."

Nick knew something. Maybe old Bill did as well. "Has someone tried to pawn it?" I asked the shopkeeper.

He shrugged. "Not 'ere. But someone could have gone to Posh Max. He trades in fancy pieces. Nobs in need of money go to 'im to 'awk their jewels."

A direction at last. "Thank you. You've both been very helpful."

"With pleasure, Miss—" Nick said, doffing his bowler.

"Harper. Mabel Harper." I flashed an innocent grin.

Nick laughed. "Sure. And Oi'm the King of England."

I bobbed him a curtsy. "Pleased to meet ye, yer highness."

"We better go, Miss," Mister Clapham said.

After I made my way to the pavement, I turned back and wiggled my fingers at Nick. It paid to be friendly with the chancier elements of society. Never knew when I'd have need of them.

CHAPTER 5

POSH MAX

*T*HE PAWNBROKER Nick had mentioned was definitely a cut above Old Bill. Not only was he dressed in much finer clothes—wool trousers, linen shirt, silk waistcoat—but he spoke with the accent of an educated man. Nick's suggestion proved correct. Posh Max had indeed been approached about the dog collar.

"Lady Elizabeth Gordon," Posh Max said. "Dressed like quality. Spoke like it too."

"Did you trade her for it?"

He scoffed. "No. I'm no pigeon to be fooled by a pretty face and manners. Not only that. Her tale was pure poppy-cock, spun from whole cloth."

"What made you think that?"

He rubbed a finger over his immaculately groomed pencil mustache. "Well, if a beloved dog died, you'd be bawling your eyes out."

Like Mrs. Grimes had.

"And she wasn't?" I asked.

"She looked like she was on her way to high tea with the queen. If she'd shed a single tear that day, I'd eat my topper." He nodded toward a bowler derby that hung on a hat rack.

"What did she look like?"

"Blonde, blue-eyed, middling height. No older than thirty, I would say. She brought a maid with her. That's another reason I didn't believe her. That servant was the one in charge, not Lady Gordon, or whatever her name is."

"Could you please explain?" It always paid to be polite.

"Well, for one thing the maid didn't remain at a respectable distance but stood right next to her mistress. Whenever Lady Gordon said something that didn't sound right, she shook her head. She was directing the whole performance with a nod or a frown."

"What did the maid look like?"

"Late thirties, thin as a rail, dark-haired, dark eyes, prune-shaped mouth. Mole high on her right cheek." He pointed to the spot on his own face. "Didn't crack a smile the whole time she was here."

"Did Lady Gordon address her at any point?"

"Aggie, she called her."

"Probably fake as well," Mister Clapham opined.

"No," Posh Max said shaking his head. "I believe that was her real name. When Lady Gordon called her that, she frowned."

I thanked Posh Max and slipped him the agreed upon amount I'd promised for his cooperation. Once we left the shop behind, I turned to Mister Clapham. "What do you think?"

He breathed out a heavy sigh. "It'll be difficult to locate them. But at least we have some descriptions to go by."

"Well, Aggie is not Gigi's nanny. Bertha Watkins couldn't be described as slender. Her hair runs closer to auburn than dark, her eyes are green, and she definitely does not have a mole on her cheek."

He got a faraway look in his eye. "Lady Gordon's description rang a bell. I've seen her before. It will come to me. By and by."

"Well, we need it soon, Mister Clapham. Mrs. Grimes has been asked to deliver the ransom money in five days' time."

CHAPTER 6

KITTY INTERVIEWS STAFF

*W*HILE MISTER CLAPHAM followed the 'Lady Gordon' lead, I returned to the Ladies of Distinction Detective Agency to change my attire. Since our enquiries often required Lady Emma and me to adopt disguises, we'd turned the townhouse's back room into an area where we stored clothing, shoes, hats, wigs, makeup. In other words, everything we needed to transform ourselves into whatever persona our investigation required. And, of course, to change back into our professional attire upon our return.

It was a good thing we'd adopted this process as there was a prospective client in the agency's reception area eager to speak to someone about a private matter. As Lady Emma had also been in absentia—she was meeting with a possible informant in the Marlowe stickpin matter—Betsy had suggested she make an appointment for another day. But the lady had decided to wait. While she did, Betsy had apparently plied her with enough tea and biscuits to sink a ship.

The last thing I wished was for her to see me dressed up as a 'tart,'as Nick had so colorfully phrased it. So, I took the time to change back into my lady detective persona.

The prospective client turned out to be Mrs. Slaynton, a middle-aged lady who suspected a staff member was stealing from her. It did not take long to take down the details, have her sign the client form, and obtain the retainer. After I assured her we would be prompt in dealing with the matter, she left satisfied. Not ten minutes after she departed, I was out the door myself for I had an appointment to interview Mrs. Grimes's staff.

Mrs. Grimes had set aside a private room for me to do so, something I'd requested to obtain the best results. Her staff consisted of Bertha Watkins, whom I'd already met, Mrs. Grimes's personal maid, both a downstairs and an upstairs maid, a housekeeper, a cook, and cook's assistant. A young man, the only male servant in the house, served as both footman and chauffeur.

I eased into the interviews by talking to Bertha Watkins first. She had nothing new to add and appeared even more worried than before. The downstairs maid, Lucy Flanagan, possessed a merry grin and mop of curls which reminded me of Betsy. She could not contribute much to the enquiry as she rarely saw Gigi. At the end of both interviews, I asked them to sign their names on a sheet of paper. Bertha Watkins was wary of doing so. But when I explained I was legally required to do so, she acquiesced. Lucy Flanagan posed no problem and happily signed.

The upstairs servant, Pamela Sweetins, was quite the opposite. The bitter, young woman complained the entire time. "Mrs. Grimes keeps that mutt with her at all times. Sheds all over the place. I'm constantly sweeping up hairs and cleaning up after it. And the smell! Stinks to high heaven, she does."

"I thought Gigi had a personal groomer."

"Who visits every ten days. In between, it's my job to give Gigi a bath, and she bites. Nasty old thing." She shoved up her right sleeve and showed me a red mark on her arm. "She loves to nip at me, the beast. I didn't sign up for that. I'm looking for another position, I am."

"Well, yes, but—"

Miss Sweetins was not finished with her tirade. Crossing her arms across her chest, she said, "It should be that old cow's job to clean up after that mutt, not mine."

"And who might that, er, old cow be?"

"Bertha Watkins. Who else? She claims she can't do it because of her bad back. Ha! Bad back indeed. She seemed mighty limber the other day when she was getting a proper rogering at midnight in the kitchen pantry. And with Donovan, no less."

Goodness! Did servants really do that? And in the kitchen no less? That couldn't possibly be sanitary. "Do you mean the footman?" I'd been provided with a list of the employees, but I needed to clarify who she meant.

"Who else? He's the only man on staff. Why, he's twenty years younger than her!"

"When did this take place?"

"Saturday last."

Three days before. "Did you actually see them enjoying, er, carnal relations?"

"No. But I heard them. She kept calling out his name. Her moans were loud enough to wake the dead, they were. If you ask me, they planned it together."

"Gigi's kidnapping, you mean."

"Yes."

Clearly, an insinuation. But was it true? "Do you have any

knowledge of such plans? Did you hear something or see something?"

"No. But it stands to reason, doesn't it?"

Her tale could be true, or it could be spun from whole cloth. I would need to find out. "I will investigate your allegations, Miss Sweetins."

"Good." A nasty grin spread over her thin lips.

I'd seen such an expression before in investigations involving domestic staff. Those who'd had a falling out often resorted to spreading false rumors in an attempt to get someone in trouble. More often than not such vitriol ended with the gossip monger being dismissed. Leaving that issue aside, I turned the interview in another direction. "What were you doing in the kitchen that late at night?"

"Toothache. Came to get some cloves. They help with the pain. Cook keeps her spices in a cupboard right next to the stove."

A reasonable explanation. I would need to verify that information with the house cook. As she had nothing else to contribute, I thanked Miss Sweetins so she could return to her duties. None too happily, I might say.

Rather than interview the footman next, I continued with my planned order, leaving him for last. There were no surprises from any of the other staff members. None appeared to have anything to do with the dognapping.

Nattily dressed in a dark blue coat, blue and silver waistcoat, and matching trousers, Thomas Donovan entered the room with a jaunty air about him. His blonde hair had a marvelous sheen to it, not a curl out of place. Handsome and he knew it.

"Thank you for talking to me, Mister Donovan."

He beamed me a dazzling smile. "Thomas will do, Miss. Everyone calls me that. We're a right friendly household."

I had to wonder how 'friendly' he was with the female

staff. Did he entertain more than one in the kitchen pantry? One on Tuesdays and another one on Thursdays? But that was neither here nor there at the moment. I had a job to do. Adopting my professional voice, I said, "I prefer to keep it a bit more formal, if you don't mind."

"Whatever you like, Miss. I'm easy to please," he said winking at me.

As if I would fall for such an obvious ploy. "By now you've heard about Gigi being kidnapped at the park."

"Of course. Who hasn't?"

"Any idea who took her?"

"No. Why would I?"

"You might have mentioned it to someone, say, an acquaintance? Seeing how Gigi's diamond dog collar is worth a small fortune, it might be worth a conversation or two at your local pub."

The grin vanished as his complexion paled. "I had nothing to do with it."

I shot him a smile, as charming as the one he'd directed at me. "Of course not, Mister Donovan. I was just speculating."

He ran a finger under his collar as if it was suddenly too tight.

"Where were you when the dog was stolen?"

"Here. Where else would I be?" He'd turned wary as his former charm faded.

"Where in particular?"

"By the door. That's my station. I sit there all day waiting for guests." He shrugged. "Not that there are many."

"You were there when the ransom note was delivered?"

"Yes. No." He contradicted himself which he soon clarified. "Call of nature. I'd temporarily stepped away."

"How very unfortunate. You could have seen who delivered it."

I couldn't very well ask him if he was in the habit of

entertaining one of the staff in the pantry. At least not until I had verified some other things. For now, I had no choice but to give him the benefit of the doubt. At the end of the interview, he didn't hesitate to sign his name on the sheet of paper. I intended to compare all the signatures to the handwriting on the ransom note. I didn't expect any to match, but I wouldn't have been doing my job if I didn't.

Once I was finished, Mrs. Grimes asked me to step into her parlor as she was eager to hear if I'd discovered anything new. I had a working theory, but not one I could share. So I gave her my standard reply. Some avenues of enquiry had opened up which I intended to follow.

I rushed back to the agency where I hoped Mister Clapham would be waiting for me. Hopefully, with news of 'Lady Gordon.' I would need to investigate not only Bertha Watkins and Donovan, but also the rest of the staff. As I'd learned early on from Mister Clapham, it was wrong to assume facts before they could be verified.

CHAPTER 7

MISTER CLAPHAM COMES UP ACES

I ARRIVED AT THE AGENCY just before we closed up for the day. As I'd hoped, Mister Clapham was there waiting for me. He'd remembered where he'd seen 'Lady Gordon' before.

"She's no lady, but an actress," he said following me into my office. "Her name is Kate Vaughn. Several years ago, she played one of the stepsisters in *Cinderella* at the Drury Lane Theatre."

I grinned. "How very splendid of you to recall that, Mister Clapham."

Betsy knocked on the open door. "Sorry to interrupt, Miss. Would you like some coffee?"

"Yes, thank you, Betsy." It was another blustery kind of day. A warm beverage would be welcomed.

"What about you, Mister Clapham?"

"Same. Thank you, Betsy."

"Does Miss Vaughn still perform?" I asked the former Scotland Yard detective inspector.

"I asked some questions around Covent Garden. From what I've learned, no. She was a bit long in the tooth to play the part of a young girl. Now, she can't even get some of the more mature roles. So she offers her services to those who need someone to play a part. Whatever it requires, she's game."

"Interesting. What about the maid?"

"Her older sister, Aggie. She worked as the wardrobe mistress for the same theatre company that employed her sister. It was steady work as the company was very popular. But three months ago, she was dismissed. Too fond of the bottle from what I hear."

I curled a brow. "With neither sister earning a regular income, life must be hard for them."

"That it is. They've been reduced to a rather bleak hand-to-mouth existence now that Kate's acting gigs have dried up as well."

"Turning them desperate enough to do something illegal?" I asked.

"Apparently so. Word on the street is they don't ask too many questions. If there's coin to be earned, they're game."

Betsy arrived with coffee service for two and a plate stacked with sweet biscuits filled with raspberry jam.

"Ooh, Jammie Dodgers, my favorites. Is this today's delivery from the bakery?"

"Yes, Miss."

"Absolutely smashing. Thank you, Betsy. You're a treasure." She was indeed a valuable asset to the agency. Not only did she greet clients, but she was a grand brewer of tea and coffee. I don't know what we would have done without her.

"You're welcome, Miss." After a quick bob, she walked out closing the door behind her.

"So someone hired them to pawn the dog's collar?" I asked Mister Clapham after we'd enjoyed sips of the excellent brew and a Jammie Dodger each.

"That's my guess. Probably for a cut of whatever they get." He bit into another biscuit. "I suggest you inform Inspector Crawford. At the very least, there's enough evidence to interrogate them."

I shook my head. "I promised Mrs. Grimes I wouldn't contact the police," I responded.

"The ransom is due in five days, Miss Worthington."

"Well, then that gives us five days to find Gigi. Did you find out where they live?"

"I did. They rent rooms above The Fox and Hound, a tavern in the Strand near Covent Garden."

I bit down on my lip.That would be a perfect place to start.

He whooshed out a hard sigh.

"What's wrong?" I asked.

"I don't like that look in your eyes."

"What look?" I batted my lashes, in my best innocent-as-a-lamb manner.

"The one that spells trouble. I've seen it before. More than once, I might add."

He was right. But then he was excellent at reading body language. "You weren't planning on doing anything tonight, were you?"

His shoulders slumped. "I gather we're going to Covent Garden."

I widened my smile in response.

CHAPTER 8

THE FOX AND HOUND

*G*IVEN THE RESTRICTIONS on pub hours which required them to close at ten, Mister Clapham and I decided to meet at eight at the Ladies of Distinction Detective Agency and proceed from there. It wasn't the first time we'd gone adventuring, nor I dared say would it be the last. Since we would need to fit in with a less than fashionable crowd, we'd dressed in clothes that wouldn't attract undue attention. Mister Clapham had topped his salt-and-pepper hair with a workman's cap, and his shirt, trousers, and coat had seen better days. Whereas for me, my skirt and blouse, finds at the secondhand store Betsy had introduced me to, were serviceable but nothing fancy. The hat I'd popped over my dark hair had delusions of grandeur. But its drooping peacock feather and bent rim spoke of someone hard on their luck.

Our arrival at the Fox and Hound largely went unnoticed, exactly what we desired as we wished to fit in. As expected, the public house was brimming with a mixture of workmen in worn clothes, ladies in various stages of dress, some more revealing than others, and, according to Mister Clapham, an assortment of ruffians, scalawags, and ne'er do wells.

After Mister Clapham spotted Aggie on the far side of the room, we chose a strategically placed table close to her. As soon as we sat, a waitress approached. Her off-the-shoulder blouse showed quite a bit of her charms which she fully put on display when she leaned forward. Ignoring me, she gave *all* her attention to Mister Clapham. No doubt the beard he was sporting and scar identified him as a successful fellow. To her dismay, he had no interest in what she was selling, but simply ordered two tankards of ale for us.

Aggie was not drinking alone. An older woman sat next to her, sipping away at her brew while Aggie bent her ear.

"We had a plan all worked out. And now she's done a bunker. With a bloke, no less."

"Left you in the lurch, she has?" The woman asked.

"We were this close" —Aggie pinched two fingers together— "to getting the job done. But now?" She blew out a breath. "What am I supposed to do, Dolly?"

"Couldn't you do it yourself, love?" Dolly asked.

"The job needs a looker, someone with a posh accent. Katie had that and more. Don't know what's going to happen, I don't. Himself is not going to be happy, I can tell you that much." She guzzled down a quarter of her ale. Having done so, she wiped the foam off her upper lip with her sleeve.

Mister Clapham and I exchanged a glance. I nodded, the predetermined signal we'd arranged between us. He would take the lead, and I'd follow.

He came to his feet and walked the two steps between our table and the one Aggie and her friend occupied. "Forgive me, but I couldn't help but overhear your plight."

"Did you now?" Aggie asked with a sneer. "What is it to you?"

"I would like to explain," Mister Clapham answered with a charming smile. "Mind if I take a seat?"

"Suit yourself." Aggie shrugged. Somewhat drunkenly, I might say.

"Thank you." He pulled out the empty chair at their table and accommodated himself. "My name is Bill. Bill Withers."

Aggie pointed a thumb to herself and her friend. "Aggie and this is Dolly."

"Pleased to meet you, ladies."

"Oooh, such nice airs about ye," Dolly said, with a cheeky grin. Clearly, she liked the look of Mister Clapham.

Aggie, however, did not as she flashed another sneer. "Fancy yerself a gent, do you?"

"I'm more of a theatrical agent," he clarified with a smile.

Aggie gave him a thorough once over. "Never seen ye before, and I've been in the business fifteen years."

"I'm from out of town. Only recently arrived. Miss Mabel Harper here" —he nodded toward me— "got tired of working the circuit. Too much traveling. She wants to settle in one place. We thought to try her luck in the city."

Aggie barked out a laugh. "She and every other provincial. The competition is quite keen. Only the best are hired."

"We're making the rounds at the moment. Mabel has sparked some interest. But nothing has come through just yet. In the meantime, we're open to other opportunities."

Aggie allowed her gaze to roam over me. "Doesn't appear to have been too successful at acting going by what she's wearing."

"Well, we didn't want to stand out. The area being what it is. I'm sure you understand."

Aggie sniffed. "You have a point."

The waitress returned. "Another round?"

"Nah," Aggie said while gazing longingly at her empty tankard.

"Please allow me," Mister Clapham said flashing a pound note. "Yes, another round, my good woman."

"Oh, ta," Dolly batted her eyelashes at Mister Clapham. "A proper gentleman, ye are."

Mister Clapham flashed his patented grin. "My pleasure, Miss Dolly."

"Your bird there" —the waitress nodded toward me —"is taking up a table by her lonesome. We got people waiting for an empty one."

"We can easily remedy that problem," Mister Clapham said before turning to me. "Mabel, join us."

"Be glad to Mister Withers." Putting on my best airs, I sauntered to Aggie's table. "Ladies," I nodded toward Aggie and Dolly, "A pleasure to meet you. I'm Mabel Harper." As I joined them, a man wrapped his arms around Aggie's companion, "Dolly, girl. You're a sight for sore eyes."

Dolly grinned up at him. "Bernie, love. Ye back in town?"

"Yes, and eager to see me Dolly girl, if you know what I mean." He squeezed her tight.

With a cheeky grin, Dolly elbowed him. "Get on with ye."

"Have ye had yer supper?"

"Not yet. Ye buying?"

"I got a table over there." He pointed somewhere behind him. "Ordered bangers and mash. Join me."

"Oh, ta. See you later, Aggie." And with that Dolly sauntered off with her fellow.

"That man's nothing but trouble," Aggie said. "He's only after one thing. Once she gives it to him, he'll drop her like a hot potato." But she ended her tirade in a somewhat wistful tone.

I wondered if Aggie had ever had a fellow want that one thing from her.

The waitress returned with three fresh tankards of ale. I intended to sip on mine. Last thing I needed was to get bosky. I needed to keep a clear head.

"So, Miss Aggie," Mister Clapham said, "you're in need of someone who can play the part of a lady? Mabel can do that."

Aggie, by now three sheets to the wind, blinked slowly at me. "Can you speak like a lady?" she asked, slurring her words.

"Of course."

"Well, say something. A speech from one of your plays."

When my sisters and I were young we would dress up and play all kinds of roles. Pirates and princesses, knights and knaves. But of course, none of those speeches would do. So I obliged by offering part of a monologue from *Lady Windermere's Fan*, a favorite play of mine.

"And yet, which is the worst, I wonder, to be at the mercy of a man who loves one, or the wife of a man who in one's own house dishonours one?"

I finished by adding a sigh at the end.

"Decent," Aggie said. "You got nice clothes? What you're wearing won't do."

"Absolutely," I said with a cheery smile, "a whole trunkful."

"So what's the job?" Mister Clapham asked.

Aggie scooted her chair closer to him and lowered her voice. "Need to get a sparkler pawned. Katie and I visited three shops. None would trade with us. But yesterday, I got a lead on another one."

"And what will Mabel be required to do?"

"She will need to dress as a lady, act like a lady, speak like a lady."

"So the job will require her to visit the shop and get the sparkler pawned?"

She cackled. "There are no flies on you, Bill!"

Time I contributed my bit. "Pawn shops won't take something just because you have something of value. There has to be a story behind it. I need to know why I'm letting go of it. Am I a widow hard on her luck?"

"Hardly! The sparkler's a dog collar. Encrusted with diamonds on a gold setting."

Mister Clapham whistled. "Someone put a gewgaw like that on a dog?"

"Yeah. A wealthy widow. She treats that bitch like it was her own child."

She could only have learned that from someone inside Mrs. Grimes's house. And that meant there was an inside informant. But who was it? We would need to find out. In the meantime, I would need to learn as much as I could from Aggie. "So why am I pawning it?"

"The dog died."

My breath hitched. Had they killed Gigi? "The dog isn't really dead, is it?"

"Of course not. The blighter who took her needs her alive so he can exchange her for the ransom."

"So what's in it for Mabel?" Mister Clapham asked.

"Twenty guineas, if and when you get the money from the pawn shop."

"How much are we asking for the collar?" I asked.

"Five hundred pounds. It's worth six times that amount."

"Are we visiting a shop that trades with the upper crust?" Mister Clapham asked.

"You're a sharp one, aren't you? Yes, we are. Posh Max turned us down but there's another one that trades with the nobs. And he's not too choosy about what he takes."

"You didn't visit him before?"

"Couldn't." She guzzled down the last of her ale. "He knows my sister in the biblical sense if you know what I mean."

Oh, yes, I knew. "Does he know you?"

"No. He never met me. That's enough jibber-jabber. Come back tomorrow at ten. I live in the rooms above this pub. Use the back stairs. And then we'll see if you can do better than Katie."

"So, where's the sparkler?" I asked.

"Think I'm going to tell you? Go on with you!"

CHAPTER 9

AGGIE'S TROUBLES

*T*HE NEXT MORNING promptly at ten Mister Clapham and I arrived at Aggie's rooms. I knocked on the door. When she didn't answer, I jiggled the knob, and the door swung wide open. The place looked a right mess. Two chairs had been upended. The sole mattress had been thrown to the floor. A wardrobe had been breached as well; its contents strewn about the room. The chest of drawers looked like it'd been rifled through as well. Whoever had done this hadn't missed a thing.

Unfortunately, Aggie wasn't there.

"Oy, you looking for Aggie?" A dark-haired woman yelled from the street.

As we had no wish to conduct this conversation in public, we took the stairs back down to the ground.

"Yes," I said once we'd reached the woman.

She propped a fist on her hip. "Coppers took her early this morning. Put up quite a fight did old Aggie. Had to put handcuffs on her. Don't know what they were looking fer, but they tossed the place."

"Thank you for telling us." Mister Clapham slipped her a pound note before we walked away.

Turning to him, I said, "Now what?"

"We contact Inspector Crawford. See why Aggie was arrested."

Telephoning would be better, but we would have to return to the agency to make that call and time was of the essence. So we hopped in a taxicab and headed for Scotland Yard. Thankfully, Robert was there and available to talk to us.

"Catherine," he said kissing my cheek. "Clapham," he shook the former inspector's hand. "To what do I owe the pleasure?"

"Something's come up in connection with the kidnapping of the poodle."

He nodded.

I told him about last night's events and what we'd discovered this morning.

"So, Miss Vaughn has been arrested?" he asked.

"Apparently."

"Umm, I haven't heard anything about it. But then I'm not privy to everything that happens at the Yard. Let me see what I can find out. Do you wish me to telephone you when I do?"

"Do you mind if we wait? We're on a rather tight schedule. The ransom is supposed to be paid in four days."

"No, of course not. Excuse me." He walked to the door and spoke to the sergeant who'd escorted us to his office before returning to us.

"Sergeant Willard will get the details. Should be back in a few minutes. In the meantime, may I offer you some tea?"

He'd barely had time to heat up the water before the

sergeant returned. He and Robert conferred in the corridor outside the office.

Once Robert learned what the sergeant had to say, he said, "Agnes Vaughn was indeed arrested last night."

"For what?"

"Stolen goods. Some of the items from the theatre company she'd worked for have gone missing."

"They've just now issued a complaint?" I asked. "She was dismissed three months ago."

"They didn't notice the items were gone until the new costume mistress conducted an inventory," Robert explained. "Of course, suspicion fell on Miss Vaughn right away seeing how she was their last one."

"Did they find what they were looking for?"

"Missing items were found in her possession. Some of them anyway. She said she sold the rest."

After thanking Robert, Mister Clapham and I walked out of Scotland Yard. Dejected did not begin to describe me. "What do we do now? She was our only lead."

"No." He shook his head. "There's one more. Her sister."

"But we don't know where she is!"

"Leave it to me, Miss Worthington. I'll find her."

"We'll have to locate her before Scotland Yard does. She may very well have run off with some of those costumes."

CHAPTER 10

MRS. GRIMES'S GRIEF

*W*HILE MISTER CLAPHAM pursued the lead to Aggie's sister, I returned to the Ladies of Distinction Detective Agency where a summons awaited me.

"Mrs. Grimes called, Miss," Betsy said. "She sounded really upset."

No sense telephoning. I would need to see her in person. I headed to her Belgravia address where I found Mrs. Grimes prostrate with grief in her parlor with Bertha Watkins attending to her.

"What happened?"

Miss Watkins answered as Mrs. Grimes found it difficult to get a word out. "Something came in the mail."

"What was it?"

She pointed a trembling hand toward a box.

I opened it to find a pink bow drenched in blood.

"That's Gigi's," Miss Watkins said in a shaky voice.

"How do you know?"

"It was created especially for her." She pointed to the small label on the underside of the bow. "Made from the finest silk, it is. She was wearing it when she was taken. Pink is her favorite color."

How a dog could communicate such a thing was beyond me. Still, Miss Watkins vouched for the provenance of the bow, so it had to be true.

Just then Mrs. Grimes moaned. "Oh, Miss Worthington, do you think they hurt my Gigi?"

"No. They need her alive to collect their ransom." With only four days left before the ransom had to be paid, time was running out. Clearly, Mrs. Grimes could not afford any further upset. This crisis was taking such a toll on her, I feared for her well-being. "May I speak to you in private, Miss Watkins?" I asked.

"Yes, of course."

After we stepped outside the parlor, I said, "If another package or a letter arrives, please don't let her open it. You do it. Call me at the agency if it's anything related to Gigi. If I'm not there, talk to Lady Emma Carlyle, my business partner. She'll know what to do."

Miss Watkins straightened up to her full height of five foot nothing. "You can count on me, Miss Worthington. I'll make sure Mrs. Grimes doesn't see any other correspondence."

After thanking her, I headed back downstairs to make my way out. But when I arrived at the front door, the footman was not at his post. Call of nature or something else? As I needed my coat and hat before I could leave, I had no choice but to wait. He didn't appear after a reasonable amount of time, so I called out, "Hello? Mister Donovan? Where are you?"

He emerged from the room where the outer garments were kept, his blonde hair tussled, his jacket buttoned wrong.

I didn't dare gaze below his waist lest I discover his trousers weren't fastened correctly.

"May I have my things, Mister Donovan?"

"Yes, of course, Miss." He sneaked back into the coatroom. As he did, someone giggled. Honestly, the man was a shameless Casanova.

"Who's in there?" I asked when he emerged.

"Mice."

I set my mouth in a firm line. "Honestly, Mister Donovan, mice don't giggle. I want to see this person. Now." It couldn't be Bertha Watkins. I'd just left her lending comfort to Mrs. Grimes.

He thrust the coat door open. "Come on out."

Another giggle and Lucy Flanagan, the downstairs maid, emerged. A surprise. Although in retrospect, I really should have expected it.

"Hush, girl." Mister Donovan cautioned. "We're in a world of trouble."

"You won't be if you answer some questions. Last Saturday, did you tryst with Mister Donovan around midnight?"

She appeared puzzled. "Tryst?"

I would need to use plainer words. "Met him to enjoy carnal relations?"

She giggled. "I sure did."

"Where?"

"The kitchen pantry. We love to do it in different places."

"Shut your mouth, woman," Mister Donovan barked out.

Ignoring him, I asked, "What time?"

"Midnight. He was ever so lovely." She batted her eyelashes at the footman.

"Thank you for your honesty, Miss Flanagan."

"You won't tell?" Donovan asked.

"About you and Miss Flanagan, no. It has nothing to do with Gigi's disappearance."

"If I were you, I'd look to Sweetins, Miss," Lucy said.

"Why do you say that?"

"She has a cousin, rough-looking fellow. He comes to the back door sometimes. A week ago, I was in the housekeeper's pantry getting some linseed oil for the furniture. I heard them whispering. They were talking about Gigi and the time Miss Watkins takes her to the park."

"Her cousin, you say?"

"Yes."

"You wouldn't happen to know his name."

"Billy. That's what she called him."

"Why didn't you tell me this before?"

"Didn't want to get my face cut up. He goes by Billy the Butcher."

CHAPTER 11

A NEW LEAD

ITH MY NEWFOUND KNOWLEDGE, I returned to the agency to discover Mister Clapham had returned with a lead on Kate Vaughn.

"As Aggie said, she's gone off with a bloke. Brighton of all places."

"How did you find that out?"

"I questioned the woman who told us about the coppers arresting Aggie. The busybody keeps a sharp eye on the comings and goings of everyone and everything near the Fox and Hound. Yesterday, she spotted Kate Vaughn hauling a huge suitcase down the stairs. Before Kate could find a taxi-cab, she spilled the beans to her. She told her she was going to Brighton with a bloke, but first she was meeting him at his place of business."

"Was Aggie present through any of this?"

"No. Apparently, she was sleeping off the previous night's

excessive drinking. You saw how much she drank at the Fox and Hound."

If she consumed as much alcohol when she'd been employed, it was no wonder she'd been dismissed.

"Well, I got a new lead from the Belgravia townhouse." I told him what the downstairs maid had said. "Does Billy the Butcher ring any bells? Sounds like a nasty customer."

"No. But I can ask around the Yard."

"That's grand, Mister Clapham." I glanced at my wrist-watch and wasn't surprised to find it was past three. Neither Mister Clapham nor I had stopped for our luncheon. "Would you care to join me at the Tea and Tattle? We need our sustenance if we are to proceed."

"Well, the pub would be better."

"The Fox and Hound, I presume."

"Yes, we can interview the staff. Maybe they know who Kate's fella is."

We headed back there. Dressed as I was in the clothes of a well-to-do lady, I thought I would stand out like a sore thumb. But there were several individuals at the pub dressed even finer than me. It struck me as odd until I realized they were theatre folk. Always well-dressed so they could make a favorable impression.

"What will you have, ducks?" The waitress who'd waited on us last night asked.

"Two orders of fish and chips and two tankards of ale," Mister Clapham said. We might as well stay with the tried-and-true.

It proved to be the right choice. The fish and chips were amazingly good, and the ale went down a treat.

Since it was a tad slow, the waitress was willing to talk to us until things got busy again. The pound note Mister Clapham offered for any information she provided didn't hurt either.

"You know Aggie and her sister?" I asked. A silly question. Of course, she did. But one had to start somewhere.

"Aye. Aggie's in here every night. Kate not so much. She likes to put on la-di-da airs. But she comes from the same stable as Aggie so she's not fooling anyone. I know quality when oi see it. And she's not it."

"Do you know where she's gone?" I asked.

"Heard she ran off to Brighton with a bloke."

"Do you know who he is?"

"Someone she met recently. Some highfalutin fancy name. Posh something or other."

Could it be? "Posh Max?"

She nodded. "That's it."

Posh Max had lied to us.

CHAPTER 12

KATE VAUGHN

TO MY DISAPPOINTMENT, Posh Max's pawn shop was closed. A sign on the door declared he'd be gone for a week. I guessed it was true. He'd run off to Brighton with Miss Vaughn.

"Well, well, well, 'oo do we have here?" A male voice called out from the sidewalk. "Mabel Harper and her copper friend."

I turned to find the gentleman I'd met a couple of days before. "Mister Nick. Sorry, I didn't catch your last name."

He doffed his hat. "Jenkins. Nick Jenkins. A pleasure to see ye again."

I stuck out my hand, "Catherine Worthington."

He shook it and executed a small bow. "Knew you weren't no Mabel. Class, ye are." He arched a brow. "Looking for Posh Max?"

"Yes. Do you know where he's gone?" I asked.

"Went off with a bird, Oi heard."

"Could he have gone to Brighton?" I asked.

He scoffed. "Way too rich for Posh Max's blood. Heard he's holed up in the Covent Garden Palace with a blonde."

A solid lead at last. At least I hoped it would be. "Where is the hotel?"

He nodded to his right. "Down that way. A few streets over. You can't miss it."

"I know where it is," Mister Clapham said. "We'll take a taxi."

But before we hailed one, I said, "Thank you, Mister Jenkins. You've been a great help."

"Anytime, Miss Worthington," he said winking at me.

It took but ten minutes to arrive at the Covent Garden Palace. I hadn't known what to expect so I was pleasantly surprised to find a clean lobby and stylish furniture. Granted it came from the Victorian age, but it had been well maintained and polished. The desk clerk was very accommodating. Once we slipped him a pound note, he gave us the information we needed. Posh Max had been assigned a room on the third floor.

Once we arrived there, Mister Clapham pounded on the door.

"Who is it?" A masculine voice inquired from within.

"Mister Clapham and Miss Worthington. We have some questions."

"About what?"

"A private matter."

"What private matter?"

"Sir, it will be to your advantage to open the door," I said. "You don't want to conduct this conversation where anyone can overhear it."

Posh Max thrust open the door. Dressed in a black silk robe with golden dragons trailing down the front over a dark pair of trousers, he appeared somewhat worse for the wear.

The night of passion he'd probably enjoyed with Kate Vaughn had clearly taken a toll on him. But then he was not a young man.

"Hello, Max," Mister Clapham said.

"May we come in?" I asked.

"Er, I'm not quite presentable, as you can see."

"We don't mind, do we Mister Clapham?"

Before he could answer, a blonde wearing a red velvet robe wrapped around her abundant charms, her hair all over the place, sidled up behind us. More than likely, she'd been to the loo down the hall.

"Miss Vaughn, I presume?" I asked.

"Yeah, what of it?"

"My name is Catherine Worthington. This is Mister Clapham. We have some questions for you."

Her not-too-happy gaze bounced between Mister Clapham and me and then she shot a nasty look at Posh Max. "You shouldn't have opened the door, ducks."

"I couldn't have them standing in the corridor asking questions, Kate. People know me. I have a business to run."

"You might as well come in then," Miss Vaughn said, pushing her way past us.

As soon as we stepped inside, Posh Max shut the door behind us. "What questions do you have of me?"

"As you know, we're investigating the kidnapping of a poodle and the theft of a diamond collar the dog was wearing around her neck. We know Miss Vaughn visited your shop in an attempt to pawn it."

Miss Vaughn took offense to my statement. "I was hired to do a job, Miss Priss. I didn't know the choker was stolen."

Sure she didn't. "It wasn't a choker. It was a dog collar. Who hired you?"

She shrugged. "Don't know. Aggie worked with the bloke. Ask her."

"Aggie's been arrested. Apparently, she stole some costumes from the theatre company she last worked."

Kate Vaughn wrapped the red velvet robe tighter around her. "I know nothing about that."

"Given your association with the stolen costumes, as well as the sparkler, Scotland Yard is eager to find out where you are, Miss Vaughn. Mister Clapham can make a quick telephone call and get some police officers here in a right minute. Did I mention he used to work for Scotland Yard?"

She dropped all her bluster. "You wouldn't."

"I won't if you tell me what I want to know. Now, who hired Aggie?"

CHAPTER 13

TRUTH OR DECEPTION?

"*I* SWEAR I DON'T KNOW," Kate said in a panic. "Aggie never tells me anything. She just tells me what the job is, and I go do it. I didn't know the sparkler was stolen. I swear it." Tears filled her eyes. They appeared genuine, but then she was an actress. She could probably produce them on cue.

Regardless, I would need to take another tack. "Where's the sparkler?"

"I don't know. Never saw it." She shrugged, and the robe slipped down revealing one bare shoulder. Another practiced move I suspected. It worked with Posh Max who glued his gaze to the spot. Not so with Mister Clapham. He knew better.

And, of course, it had no effect on me. "So you were trying to pawn something you never saw? How did you know it was real?"

"I told you I was hired to do a job. Once we got a bite, someone would have come in and closed the deal."

"And no one took you up on the offer?"

"No. Everyone thought something was fishy. Max certainly did." The glance she directed at him was that of a pure siren. "He's so swet, and such a gentleman."

Posh Max was definitely enthralled if that mesmerized smile was anything to go by. Had he never heard of Lilith, the temptress who embodied chaos and seduction? That definitely was Kate. She was using him for some purpose. What it was we'd need to discover.

And the sooner the better. "Mister Clapham. I think it's time we called Scotland Yard."

"No!" Her suddenly-turned-hard gaze snapped to me.

"Then start telling the truth."

"All right. It was___"

Someone pounded on the door interrupting what she was about to say.

"That's our tea," Kate said. "Been waiting for it ever so long."

But when Posh Max opened the door, there was no waiter with tea service on the other side. Rather, a red-haired man stood there, a menacing look in his eye and a nasty scar down his cheek.

CHAPTER 14

BILLY THE BUTCHER

*P*USHING POSH MAX out of the way, the man strode into the room, an associate just as evil looking as him by his side.

"What do you want?" Posh Max asked in a shaky voice. He was brave I had to give him that.

The associate retrieved a revolver from his waist and pointed it toward Posh Max. "Shut yer trap."

Posh Max wisely clammed up.

Taking several steps forward until he was towering over Kate, the red-haired man asked, "Did you talk?"

She sneered. "Not bloody likely. I know better than to say anything."

So she'd known. Just as I thought, she'd been lying through her teeth.

I drew his attention next. "Who are you?"

"Catherine Worthington. I'm a private investigator. All I want is the dog. You can keep the diamond collar."

He scoffed. "That's not happening."

"Why are you here?" I asked.

"You ask too many questions," said the red-haired man. Glancing at his associate, he jerked his head toward me.

The associate raised his arm, his intent clear, but before his closed hand could connect with me, Mister Clapham stepped forward and met the brunt of his fist. He dropped to the floor, blood streaming down the side of his face.

Kneeling by his side, I called out his name, but he didn't answer. The brute had knocked him unconscious.

The violent act had been too much for Posh Max. He'd turned tail and run, seeking shelter by the opposite side of the bed. So much for his valor.

I fetched a handkerchief from my handbag and applied it to Mister Clapham's temple. I didn't like the color of his face. He'd gone deadly white. I wanted to say something, protest about the thug's brutish behavior. But I feared it would earn me the same treatment. I couldn't have that happen as I would need to provide Mister Clapham with whatever succor I could. So I kept mum.

Ignoring us, the red-haired man pointed to Kate. "You need to come with us. Himself wants to talk to you."

Both Aggie and this man had used the same word to refer to the man who more than likely planned the whole scheme. Clearly, they were all part of the same scheme.

Kate brushed a hand down her red velvet robe. "I can't go out looking like this. I need to change." No wonder. She was probably wearing nothing beneath it.

"All right, but be quick about it."

Kate grabbed a dress she'd tossed over a chair and the undergarments that went along with it. And then she disappeared behind a dressing screen that had been set up in the corner of the room. While she changed into more decent attire, I poured water from a pitcher into a porcelain basin placed on the night table next to the bed and dipped my handkerchief into it. I then applied the linen to Mister Clapham's head once more. He was still unconscious, but I'd managed to stem the blood flow.

Kate emerged from behind the screen and turned her back to me. "Could you button me up, please?"

After I did, the red-haired man asked, "You done?"

"Not yet," she said slipping into a pair of black patent leather shoes. "I need to brush my hair."

She had a point. It rather resembled a bird's nest.

It took her another few minutes to arrange it into a semblance of normality that would pass muster in public. When she made to grab her handbag, the red-haired man barked out. "Leave it."

"No." A mysterious glance passed between them. One I couldn't decipher. Whatever was inside the handbag must be something of value. Doubted it was the dog collar, though.

"Fine," the red-haired man said. He once more nodded toward the associate. Apparently, a signal for the thug to grab Kate by the arm. I thought she'd object. But, to my surprise, she acquiesced meekly enough.

"We'll be leaving now," the red-haired man said. "Don't follow us. If you do, Kate here will pay the price."

Once they walked out, I breathed a sigh of relief. I would need to contact the police, but not before Mister Clapham regained consciousness. Dipping the handkerchief once more into the water, I applied it judiciously. I was rewarded for my efforts when Mister Clapham opened his eyes.

"What happened?" He asked somewhat groggily.

"A brute hit you with his fist. How do you feel?"

"Like my face is on fire."

When he went to touch the growing bruise, I stopped him. "Don't. It might make it worse."

From his prone position, he gazed around the room. "The woman. Where did she go?"

"They took her."

"Who?"

"The red-haired man and his accomplice."

"Oh." His eyes were focused, and he was alert which meant I could do what needed to be done.

"I have to go downstairs and contact the police." There was no telephone in the room to call the lobby. "Can you manage without me for a few minutes?"

"Sure. I've suffered worse than this."

Before I rode the lift to the ground floor, I warned Posh Max not to leave. If he did, it would go badly for him. Downstairs, I informed the clerk about Kate's kidnapping and then I telephoned Robert at Scotland Yard and told him what had happened.

I returned to the hotel room to find Posh Max had changed into his usual togs, projecting the image of a gentleman once more. Mister Clapham sat on a chair holding my handkerchief to his head. I was glad to see the color of his face was no longer deadly white. By the time Robert and a squad of officers arrived, he was feeling much like his usual self. But I didn't like the purple bruise on his face. He would need to be seen by a physician.

After I gave him a quick summary of what had occurred, Robert turned to Posh Max who told him how he came to be at the hotel with Kate. Robert wanted to ask him more questions, but this was not the place to do so. So, he had him escorted to Scotland Yard to await further interrogation. Needless to say, Posh Max was not happy about it. But he went off with a police officer quietly enough.

CHAPTER 15

ANOTHER KIDNAPPING

Once Posh Max was led away, Robert, Mister Clapham, and I were free to openly discuss the matter.

"I think I know who the red-haired man is," Robert replied.

"Who?" I asked.

"Your description matches that of Scotty Woods, an associate of a nasty thug from the East End," Robert said.

I had my suspicion. Still I had to ask, "What thug?"

"Billy the Butcher."

My breath hitched. "I heard that name just today in connection with the poodle kidnapping."

His gaze widened. "Why didn't you call me as soon as you learned that?"

"Because Mrs. Grimes asked us not to contact the police about the dognapping. We had no idea it would lead to a kidnapping. Although to be honest, I'm not sure it is one."

His brow scrunched. "Why do you think that?"

"Kate Vaughn knows who arranged this whole scheme. When Scotty Woods asked her if she'd said anything, she said that she knew better. Still, they were rough with her. I didn't totally buy it, though. They could have been putting on an act for my benefit."

"For what reason?"

"To delay my contacting you. They threatened to harm her if I did. It didn't work, of course. I contacted you as soon as Mister Clapham regained consciousness."

"Maybe so, but Billy the Butcher and his gang are dangerous people. They like to mark their victims."

"Scotty Woods has a scar."

"It's not only victims they like to hurt. From what I understand, it's an initiation ritual with that gang."

I gasped. "I hope they don't do that to Kate. Aside from damaging her, she'd never get another acting job."

"Don't worry. We'll find her. We know their usual haunts." He gently cradled my shoulders. "It's late."

I gazed out the window. He was right. Night had fallen.

"There's nothing more you can do tonight. Go home, Catherine."

"Not before we stop at the hospital and have Mister Clapham seen to."

"I'm fine, Miss Worthington," Mister Clapham said.

"Sure you are," I said with a soft smile. "But it will make me feel worlds better if you're seen to by a physician."

"Better do as she asks, Clapham," Robert said. "Head injuries can have tragic consequences."

Mister Clapham breathed out a hard sigh. "Fine."

Robert bit back a smile as he addressed Mister Clapham, "I'll have a police officer drive you to St. Thomas, the closest hospital." He turned back to me. "Promise me you'll go home afterwards."

"I will. I promise."

The hospital staff was very accommodating. It took an hour for them to examine and bandage Mister Clapham. But once they'd done so, they gave him the all clear.

"I told you I was right as rain," he said as we climbed aboard a taxi outside St. Thomas.

"Well, it didn't hurt to have you examined by a doctor. I wouldn't have slept tonight worrying about you." After a brief pause, I asked, "You wouldn't like to come home with me? Just for tonight?" Heaven knew we had plenty of bedrooms. "That way we can check on you to make sure you're all right."

"Thank you, but I'll have to decline your kind offer. A lady friend is expecting me for supper."

"Oh?" He'd never mentioned a lady friend before. But then why would he? He would want to keep his private life to himself.

"She will keep an eye on me."

"That's good to hear." And with that, I had to be satisfied no matter how curious I was.

The lady friend apparently lived only a couple of streets over from him since that's where he asked the taxicab driver to take him.

My arrival at home went largely unnoticed by my family who was enjoying cocktails in the drawing room. I'd sent word from the hospital that I would be delayed, sharing the news about Mister Clapham's injury but little else. After a quick wash in my room and a change of clothes, I joined them.

"Kitty, dear, is Mister Clapham all right?" Mother asked as soon as I stepped into the room.

"Yes. It was only a bump on the head." It was more than that, but I didn't want to alarm her. "He should be right as rain by morning." Or at least I hoped he would be.

CHAPTER 16

THE MORNING AFTER

RIGHT AFTER BREAKFAST the next morning I telephoned Mister Clapham. He was already up and about, having broken his own fast. He said he was fine, and I had nothing to worry about. I didn't know about that. When I saw him at the agency later on, the entire left side of his face was one big bruise.

"You should have stayed home to rest," I suggested.

A look of horror spread over his face. "In the middle of an investigation? I think not."

The phone rang interrupting our discussion. "It's Inspector Crawford, Miss."

"Thank you, Betsy." I picked up the telephone. "Robert, did you find Kate Vaughn?"

"No. But we did find out they have your poodle. Apparently, he bit someone."

"She. It's a girl poodle."

"Well, she's a nasty customer, according to the person she

bit. She showed it to me. How could a small thing have such a big bite is beyond me."

"It's a standard poodle. That breed is not tiny."

"Well, regardless, we have a lead on where they've gone. Someone heard them mention they're headed for Chiswick. Kate Vaughn, Billy the Butcher, Scotty Woods, the dog. Apparently, the whole gang has scampered there."

"Mind if Mister Clapham and I come with you?" I asked.

"Thought you'd want to join us. I'll be there in fifteen minutes."

"Chiswick is an interesting choice for them to run to, don't you think?" I asked Robert once he arrived at the agency.

"Why do you say that?"

"That's where Kate Vaughn and Aggie are from," I said. "The more I mull it over, the more I think there's a connection between them and Billy the Butcher. Not only that but Mrs. Grimes's upstairs maid knows him as well. She reminded me of Kate, or rather Kate reminds me of her. What if they're all family?"

"And then there's Scotty Woods," Robert said, "a known associate of Billy the Butcher who showed up at the hotel supposedly to 'kidnap' Kate." He didn't believe any more than I did that Kate had been kidnapped.

"I think Billy sent his associate to fetch her once they finished what they set out to do."

"Which is what?" Robert asked.

"Well, I keep thinking about what Kate did. She talked Posh Max into renting a room at a local hotel and spent the night with him. He might be a handsome fellow, but he's too old for her."

Mister Clapham cleared his throat. "Some younger women find older gentlemen attractive, Miss Worthington.

We might not have the stamina of a young buck, but we possess a world of experience and infinitely more patience."

My face flushed with heat while Robert suppressed a grin. "Yes, well, you may be right, Mister Clapham. But Kate did not seem smitten. Just the opposite, she was rather short with him. I think she planned the stay at the hotel with Posh Max, and I have to ask myself why."

"And the answer is?" Robert asked with a raised brow.

"Well, what if Billy the Butcher wanted exclusive use of Posh Max's premises."

"For what purpose?"

"That's what I can't figure out."

"Rumor has it he breaks up the jewelry that he bargains for into smaller settings," Mister Clapham said. "Apparently, he has a work area set up in the back."

"That's it! You're brilliant, Mister Clapham. Just think of it. Billy had the collar, but he needed a place to break it into smaller pieces. No one in his right mind would buy a huge diamond collar, but they would accept something smaller, or even the diamonds by themselves. Billy the Butcher could have had the collar refashioned into bracelets, rings, what have you, with no one the wiser they'd once been part of a larger piece." I glanced at Robert. "Do you think Posh Max had anything to do with it?"

"I don't think so," Robert said. "I interrogated him at length last night. He doesn't suspect anything of that nature. Even after everything that occurred, he still believes Kate is attracted to him. Mainly because she was the one who suggested the rendezvous at the hotel."

"He's in for hard fall, I'm afraid," I said. "Did you release him?"

"Last night. I warned him to stay away from his shop until I gave him the all clear. Good thing I did, suspecting what we now do. Let me telephone the Yard before we set out. We'll need to raid the place."

Once he'd taken care of that, we set out for Chiswick. Although I suspected the remains of the dog collar would be found in Posh Max's premises, it wouldn't be whole. But we still had to find the dog.

CHAPTER 17

CHISWICK

*T*HE RIDE TO CHISWICK did not take long. Maybe half an hour once we cleared London traffic. Mister Clapham, of course, came along. He occupied the front passenger seat next to the police officer while Robert and I sat in the back. It wasn't the first time I'd been in a police vehicle. Robert had driven me home after I'd had a misunderstanding with the police.

"Any idea where we should go once we arrive in Chiswick?"

"I contacted the Chiswick constabulary. Billy's family has quite a reputation for thievery, muggings, and other crimes. Their father worked at the local brewery but apparently gave it up for a life of crime. He met a nasty end at the end of a knife one night, leaving young Billy as the sole male in the family. He followed in his father's footsteps and had quite a successful run. But when things got too hot, he scampered for the Big Smoke."

"London, you mean?"

"Yes, easier to get lost in the city. Once he found other like-minded fellows, he continued his crime spree. He has several hidey-holes. When one gets made, he moves to another. From what the Chiswick constabulary tells me, the entire family works at the enterprise. One of them must have seen that poodle with its diamond dog collar on Belgrave Square. And that would have led to the whole nefarious scheme."

"So a member of their family, Miss Nevins, gets hired as a maid to learn about the dog's routine. Once she had that, she transmitted the information to her cousin, Billy the Butcher himself."

"That had to be how it happened. They could simply have stolen the dog collar and be done. But they got greedy and demanded a ransom for Gigi. They knew the mistress was rich and loved Gigi so much she'd be willing to pay."

Once we reached the Chiswick constabulary, Robert discussed the matter with the detective inspector he'd talked to before.

"I checked around," the detective inspector said. "No one's seen Billy for months."

"What about his family?" Robert asked.

"The two daughters moved out long ago. The only one left is the mother. She's residing at home."

"Would you happen to know the daughters' names?" I asked.

"Agatha and Kate Vaughn."

"They're involved in this crime as well," I said.

"We arrested Agatha on another matter," Robert explained to the detective inspector. "Kate was taken by someone we know as Scotty Woods. We thought she'd been kidnapped, but we now suspect she's part of the scheme."

"From what you said, it was well-planned and carried

out," the detective inspector said. "So what should be our next step? We can't exactly knock on the mother's door and ask where her children are."

"You may not, but I certainly can," I said.

"For what reason?"

Once I explained my plan, they reluctantly agreed that it was a good scheme. Now all I had to do was make it work.

CHAPTER 18

MRS. VAUGHN

*A*GGIE AND KATE'S MOTHER opened the door herself. Appearing to be in her mid-sixties, she resembled the older daughter more than the younger as she had Aggie's hooked nose and Kate's blonde hair. Although it was mostly silver, I could still see threads of gold.

"Mrs. Vaughn?" I asked.

"Yes." She seemed a bit wary.

"I have news of your daughter Aggie."

"Do ye now?" she asked with an arched brow.

"Yes, may I come in?"

"Sure." She opened wide the door, and I stepped through the threshold. Although the house was tiny, it was immaculately kept. I followed her to the front room where everything was buffed to a shine. She'd obviously applied linseed oil to every stick of furniture.

"What a lovely home you have," I said. It was the truth. Clearly, she had pride of place.

"Thank ye. Please take a seat." Once we'd done so, she asked, "Now what about Aggie?"

"I'm sorry to tell you she's been arrested."

"What fer?" How strange. Her tone was more inquisitive than surprised.

"The theatre company she'd worked for laid a complaint against her with the police. Apparently, some costumes were missing."

"And you know this how?" The lady was very good at asking questions.

"I saw it happen. I was on my way to see her when the coppers pulled up in force, an entire squad of them. Unfortunately, they tossed the place."

"And Kate? Did they take her too?"

Interesting. She hadn't batted an eye when I'd told her Aggie had been arrested. But Kate was another thing altogether. "No. Apparently, she'd gone off with a gentleman. To Brighton, I heard."

A soft look bloomed across her face. "That girl always liked the sea. Used to take her there when she was little."

A sudden eruption sounded from the back of the house. Within seconds, a man joined us—big, muscular, nasty looking. Had to be the son. Bits of him resembled his mother. But he must have inherited his dark hair from his father.

"Billy. What are ye doing here?"

"Don't tell her nothing, Ma. She's with the cops."

Kate Vaughn sauntered in from behind Billy. "Well, well, well, if it isn't Miss Worthington in the flesh."

"Miss Vaughn." Coming to my feet, I glanced at all of them in turn. "Family reunion?"

"You're a sharp one, you is," Billy said.

"Where's the dog?" I asked.

"Dog? What dog?" Mrs. Vaughn said, her gaze bouncing between Billy and me.

"They kidnapped a standard poodle and are holding her for ransom," I explained. "Her mistress is devastated."

"Now why would you want to do that, Billy boy?" His mother asked.

"Money, Ma. What else? That dog's worth a fortune." He grabbed my arm. "Come on. You're coming with me."

I tossed him my most arrogant gaze. "Do you honestly think I came here by myself? There's an entire squad of police officers outside. If I don't come out in fifteen minutes, they'll storm the house."

"Billy, you let her go," Mrs. Vaughn said in a rush, clearly agitated. "I don't want my home broken into."

"Oh, Ma."

"I just want the dog, Billy. Where is she?" When he didn't answer, I explained things to him. "Look, so far all you've done is kidnap a dog and stolen a diamond collar which I presume has been broken into smaller pieces by now."

He blinked. "How did you—Never mind."

"If you tell me where the dog is, and I find her, you can slip away. You and Kate. Leave your mother and her beautiful home out of it. Tell me where Gigi is."

"Tell her, Billy," the mother said in a harsh tone. "Tell her right now."

Billy chewed his lip for a couple of seconds. And then he said, "Brewster's Brewery. The Basement."

"Is someone guarding her?"

He scoffed. "What do you think?"

Suddenly, there was a hard pounding on the door. "Open up! Police."

With little time to discover what I needed to know, I asked, "How many?"

"Two." He turned to his sister. "Come on, Kate."

"Nah. You go on. I'll take my chances with the coppers."

"Suit yourself." And then he was gone.

CHAPTER 19

BREWSTER'S BREWERY

*W*HILE KATE VAUGHN was taken into custody by the police, I relayed the information I'd learned from her brother to Robert and the Chiswick detective inspector.

"Brewster's Brewery, you say," the detective inspector confirmed.

"Yes. They're keeping Gigi in the basement."

"We'll take it from here," Robert said.

"I'd like to—"

"No," he responded before I finished.

I frowned. "You don't even know what I was going to say."

"Yes, I do. You want to be part of the raid on the brewery. I can't allow that to happen. Billy the Butcher's gang will have weapons, Catherine. It will be downright dangerous."

"You allowed me to question Mrs. Vaughn." I pointed out. Never mind she was standing but a few feet away.

Robert lowered his voice. "She doesn't have a history of violence. Her son does. Surely, you see that?"

"I'd still like to come." Before he could dismiss my suggestion, I rushed to say, "To observe."

He whooshed out a breath. "Very well. You can observe from a police car."

"Best do as he says, Miss Worthington," Mister Clapham said. "You don't want Inspector Crawford worrying about you. He might get hurt himself if he has to watch over you."

Mister Clapham had a point. "Fine. I'll sit in a police vehicle while you have all the fun."

Robert bit back a smile.

As it turned out, Brewster's Brewery was not far from Mrs. Vaughn's home. The Chiswick superintendent met them there. He'd been alerted to the raid by a police officer sent by the detective inspector. The three of them put their heads together and came up with a plan. While the superintendent would enter through the brewery's front entrance, Robert and the detective inspector would lead two different squads through the back and side entrances.

Mister Clapham did not join them as he was still feeling the effects of his beating. Rather than remain within the vehicle, I stepped outside. The day was too glorious to be cooped up. As Mister Clapham and I were discussing the loose ends of the investigation, such as the dog collar, I heard the mad barking of a dog. And it was not coming from inside the brewery.

"Could be any dog," Mister Clapham said glancing at me.

"Wouldn't hurt to look."

"You were told to stay put."

Disregarding his warning, I headed toward a structure on the side of the building from where the barking emanated. It appeared to be a storage shed. As we approached, the barking grew even more frenzied.

"What are you going to do?" Mister Clapham asked. "Kick down the door?" he asked, half in jest.

"There must be a window." Sure enough, I soon found one. Dirt encrusted as it was, I hoped I could see through it. Sneaking up to it, I peeked inside. The two men inside were the same ones who'd come to the hotel, one of which Robert had identified as Scotty Woods. He stood in the center of the space smoking a cigarette. The dark-haired man who hit Mister Clapham was seated on a rickety-looking chair. His right leg sported a bandage through which blood had seeped through. A white standard poodle tied on a very short leash to a table bared her teeth at the man with the bandaged leg. She'd probably bitten him. Good on you, Gigi.

I nodded to Mister Clapham and held up two fingers. As we were discussing quietly what to do, one of the police officers spotted us. I summoned him over while keeping my fingers over my lips, a signal to approach us quietly. Thankfully, he complied. Even better, he had a cudgel.

In a low voice, I explained my plan. After he nodded his understanding, I knocked on the door to the shed. "Open up. It's me, Kate."

Someone inside unlocked the door and thrust it open. "About tim—" he didn't get to finish the word as I'd stepped aside. The police officer rushed in and knocked him out with his cudgel. Before the other man could rise to his feet, Mister Clapham batted him on the head. Grinning back at me, Mister Clapham said, "Payback."

Yes, it was certainly that. Both thugs had been vanquished in the space of ten seconds.

Not knowing who was friend or foe, Gigi growled and bared her teeth. But I'd come prepared.

Fetching the handkerchief I'd obtained from Mrs. Grimes on which many of her tears had been shed, I waved it under Gigi's snout. "I'm here to rescue you, Sweetheart." As soon as

Gigi got a whiff of the scent, she whined. Poor thing had been grieving over her mistress as much as Mrs. Grimes had been grieving for her.

I loosened the knot that had chained her to the table and made to leave when Robert rushed in. "You found her!"

"There are no flies on you, Inspector." I softened my words with a grin.

A couple of police officers who had followed him put Scotty Woods and his accomplice in handcuffs. I watched with pleasure as they were led away.

"Did you find Billy?"

"Yes."

"Where was he?"

"In his mother's house. He never left. That's why we discussed our plans in front of his mother. Once she saw us leaving, she rushed to tell Billy. A couple of police officers who'd stayed behind followed her. Needless to say, Billy was not apprehended easily."

"Where was he hiding?"

"The basement. There's a secret room down there. He could have stayed hidden for weeks. How did you discover where the dog was hidden?"

"I heard Gigi barking."

Hearing her name, she jumped on me with excitement. I couldn't have that. She'd ruin my dress. In no uncertain terms, I ordered, "Sit!"

She sat, and after that, she was meek as a lamb.

CHAPTER 20

A HAPPY ENDING

*I*T WAS EARLY EVENING by the time Mister Clapham and I reached Mrs. Grimes's Belgravia home. Although Robert would have loved to join us, he needed to head to Scotland Yard to process Billy the Butcher and his gang.

"Oh, Gigi, you're home," Mrs. Grimes said while tears rained down her face. Once she'd bestowed numerous kisses on her beloved pooch, and received quite a few in return, she glanced up at me. "I don't know how I'll ever thank you, Miss Worthington. Wherever did you find her?"

"In an Ipswich brewery. Is your upstairs maid around?" That was something that needed to be handled.

"No," Mrs. Grimes said. "She resigned this morning. Rather suddenly, I might add."

"Good riddance," Bertha Watkins said, folding her arms across the middle. "She was nothing but trouble."

"Why did you want to see her?" Mrs. Grimes asked.

"More than likely she provided the information that led to Gigi being taken," I explained. "Do you have any idea where she's gone?"

"No," Bertha Watkins said. "She didn't leave a forwarding address. She simply cleared out."

"No matter. The police will find her," I said. "She and her kin are responsible for a number of crimes, not the least of which is Gigi's kidnapping and the theft of her diamond collar."

By now Mrs. Grimes had stopped listening to me. All her attention was showered on Gigi. "My sweet girl needs a bath after what those nasty people did to her." She glanced toward Bertha Watkins. "Let's call her groomer and have him attend to her right away."

A look of relief swept over Miss Watkins's face. Poor thing probably thought she'd be expected to perform the task. "Right away, Mrs. Grimes." With that, she stepped out of the room presumably to make that telephone call.

After such an eventful day, all I wanted was my own bath and a bit of a lie down. So I went home and did just that.

***

It wasn't until the next evening that I heard from Robert. But then I hadn't expected to. His duties at Scotland Yard would have claimed his time.

I descended the Worthington House staircase eager to join my family for cocktails in the drawing room. To my great surprise and elation, Robert was there talking with Father and my brother, Ned.

As soon as I made my entrance, he excused himself and strolled toward me.

"Catherine. You look lovely." He kissed my cheek.

The greeting, tame as it was, stirred my senses. But then, when didn't he do so? "Thank you."

Our butler Carlton approached with my usual drink of choice, a side car, which I acknowledged with a thank you. As Robert had his own whiskey in hand, we headed toward a settee in the far side of the room where we could hold a private conversation.

I was dying to know how everything had gone at Scotland Yard. "Did you get everyone processed?" I asked taking a seat.

"Those we could find," he said joining me. "We have the mastermind. That's the most important thing."

"Billy?"

"Mrs. Vaughn. He was the muscle. She was the brains."

Well, that was a surprise. "But she seemed so sweet!"

"She isn't. That secret room in the basement? That's where she locked up her children when they misbehaved. Apparently, Billy spent a great deal of time there."

"No wonder he's so violent. I almost feel sorry for him."

"From what Kate Vaughn shared, she and Agatha left the house as soon as they could. But their mother wouldn't allow Billy to leave. He was her sole provider. We found a trunkful of ill-gotten gains in that basement room as well."

No wonder Kate chose to be arrested by the police. Once the jig was up, the last thing she'd have wanted was to remain in that house. "You arrested Mrs. Vaughn then?"

"At the same time we did Billy."

"What about his gang?"

"They're all singing like canaries. It'll take a while to work out who did what and when, but it's fair to say Billy the Butcher's gang will be imprisoned for a long time."

"And to think it all started with the kidnapping of a dog."

He sipped from his whiskey glass. "Is your client happy with the result?"

I grinned. "She's ecstatic. Before I left her Belgravia home, she mentioned she would add a bonus to our fee. What about the dog collar? Did the police find it?"

"Posh Max's premises were indeed employed to break it apart. We consulted a master jeweler. There's no hope it can be repaired. Mrs. Grimes will have to buy a new one."

"I pressed upon her the importance of Gigi sporting an ordinary one. She agreed to follow my advice. She's also hiring a security guard."

"For the dog?"

"And her residence. That house is just begging to be burgled. She asked us to find one for her. Mister Clapham will be conducting the interviews."

"Maybe you should go into the house security business."

"Finding guards, you mean?"

"And finding weaknesses in a house. Clapham has a great deal of expertise in that area. He can perform inspections and suggest measures they could take to prevent someone breaking in."

"That's an excellent thought, Robert. I'll mention it to Mister Clapham in the morning."

"My dears." Mother stood in front of us, a soft smile on her face.

"Yes, Mother," I said while Robert came to his feet.

"Carlton has announced supper. But you were so engrossed in your conversation you may not have heard him."

"My apologies, Mrs. Worthington," Robert said. "I was relating to Kitty the details surrounding the capture of Billy the Butcher's gang."

Mother shook her head. "Such an unfortunate name. May I make a suggestion, Robert dear?"

"Of course," he said.

"It might be better to defer your discussion to another

time." She pointed to the other people in the room. "Your friends and family would love to discuss pleasanter topics with you."

The gentlest of rebukes, but then that was Mother.

Robert bowed. "We would be glad to do so. Wouldn't we, Catherine?" He asked glancing back at me.

If I knew my friends, and I did, they were dying to learn all about the arrest of Billy the Butcher and his gang. But who was I to disappoint Mother?

Offering her a smile, I stood up as well. "Of course, Mother. We'll be happy to oblige."

And then Robert and I, along with everyone else, proceeded to supper where not a word was spoken about Billy the Butcher and his nefarious pursuits.

IF YOU WOULD LIKE to read more Kitty Worthington's and Lady Emma's adventures, check out the next book in the series, **The Case of the Stray Stickpin.**

LONDON. **1923**. When Lord Marlowe's jewel-encrusted stickpin goes missing at his gentlemen's club, he seeks the services of Lady Emma Carlyle to find it for him. It's not just any old stickpin, mind you, but a family heirloom which his late father gifted to him.

Lady Emma is more than happy to take the case as the Ladies of Distinction Detective Agency's finances are shaky at best. With wit, charm, and not a small amount of daring, Lady Emma navigates the complex social hierarchy of the club. As she delves into the exclusive world of the club's members, she discovers a tapestry of intrigue, jealousy, and hidden agendas that lie beneath the veneer of gentility.

Unwilling to stand aside, Lord Marlowe insists on helping with the enquiry. As they spend more time together, the chemistry that exists between them puts the investigation at risk. Before long, the case takes an unexpected turn and hidden secrets come to light. And when the line blurs between professional duty and her personal needs, Lady Emma makes a careless mistake. One with drastic consequences.

The Case of the Stray Stickpin, Book 2 in the Kitty Worthington Cozy Capers, is another delightful historical cozy mystery. Set in the glamorous world of 1920s London, it's sure to delight readers of lighthearted historical cozy mysteries.

HAVE you read the first Kitty Worthington Mystery? **Murder on the Golden Arrow**, Book 1 in the Kitty Worthington Mysteries, is available on Amazon and Kindle Unlimited

WHAT'S **a bright young woman to do when her brother becomes the main suspect in a murder? Why, solve the case of course.**

England. 1923. After a year away at finishing school where she learned etiquette, deportment, and the difference between a salad fork and a fish one, Kitty Worthington is eager to return home. But minutes after she and her brother Ned board the Golden Arrow, the unthinkable happens. A woman with a mysterious connection to her brother is poisoned, and the murderer can only be someone aboard the train.

When Scotland Yard hones on Ned as the main suspect, Kitty sets out to investigate. Not an easy thing to do while juggling the demands of her debut season and a mother intent on finding a suitable, aristocratic husband for her.

With the aid of her maid, two noble beaus, and a flatulent basset hound named Sir Winston, Kitty treads a fearless path through the glamorous world of high society and London's dark underbelly to find the murderer. For if she fails, the insufferable Inspector Crawford will most surely hang a noose around her brother's neck.

A frolicking historical cozy mystery filled with dodgy suspects, a dastardly villain, and an intrepid heroine sure to win your heart. **Murder on the Golden Arrow** is available on Amazon and Kindle Unlimited.

CAST OF CHARACTERS

Kitty Worthington - Our amateur sleuth

The Ladies of Distinction Detective Agency
Lady Emma Carlyle - Agency Partner
Betsy Robson - Agency Receptionist
Owen Clapham - former Scotland Yard detective inspector who assists with investigations

The Grimes Household
Mrs. Grimes - Agency Client and Gigi's owner
Bertha Watkins - Gigi's Nanny
Pamela Sweetins - Upstairs Maid
Lucy Flanagan - Downstairs Maid
Thomas Donovan - Footman

Other Notable Characters
Detective Inspector Robert Crawford - Kitty's fiancé
Lord Marlowe - An Earl
Old Bill - Pawn Shop Owner
Posh Max - Pawn Shop Owner

Nick Jenkins - Pawn Shop Customer

Aggie Vaughn - Former Theatre Company Wardrobe Mistress

Lady Elizabeth Gordon - Customer at Posh Max's Pawn Shop

Kate Vaughn - Former Actress

Mrs. Vaughn – Mother to Aggie and Kate Vaughn

ISBN-13: (EBook) 978-1-943321-25-4

ISBN-13: (Print) 978-1-943321-30-8

Hearts Afire Publishing First Edition: September 2023

Made in the USA
Las Vegas, NV
12 October 2023

78953731R00052